Gram's Song

Illustrated by
Bill Farnsworth

BEST-SELLING AUTHOR
KARYN HENLEY

Tyndale House Publishers, Inc.
Wheaton, Illinois

To all children, young and old,
who have lost someone special:

There is a time for everything, and a season for every activity under heaven: a time to be born and a time to die, a time to plant and a time to uproot . . . a time to weep and a time to laugh, a time to mourn and a time to dance.

Ecclesiastes 3:1-2, 4, NIV

Visit Tyndale's exciting Web site at www.tyndale.com

Copyright © 2003 by Karyn Henley. All rights reserved.

Exclusively administered by Child Sensitive Communication, LLC.

For permission to copy excerpts from this book, contact Tyndale House Publishers, Inc., Wheaton, Illinois 60187.

Cover and interior illustrations copyright © 2003 by Bill Farnsworth. All rights reserved.

Edited by Betty Free Swanberg

Designed by Beth Sparkman

Scripture quotation is taken from the *Holy Bible,* New International Version®. NIV®. Copyright © 1973, 1978, 1984 by International Bible Society. Used by permission of Zondervan Publishing House. All rights reserved.

"Gram's Song" Words and music by Karyn Henley ©2003 Chatterville Music Co. (ASCAP) All rights reserved. Used by permission.

 Music Co. (ASCAP) All rights reserved. Used by permission.

Library of Congress Cataloging-in-Publication Data

Henley, Karyn.

 Gram's song / author, Karyn Henley.

   p. cm.

Summary: Anthony enjoys spending time with his grandmother, so when she dies he is sad until his mother tells him that Gram is now with Jesus, and reminds him of the treasures she left him, including her special song.

 ISBN 0-8423-7669-0

 [1. Death—Religious aspects—Fiction. 2. Grandmothers—Fiction. 3.

Christian life—Fiction.] I. Title.

 PZ7.H3895 Gr 2003

 [E]—dc21

            2002014267

Printed in China

09 08 07 06 05 04 03

7   6   5   4   3   2   1

MESSAGE TO PARENT OR TEACHER

One of the most difficult tasks an adult might face is talking to a child about death, especially the death of someone the child knew and loved. If you are faced with this task, understand that one conversation will not resolve all of a child's questions. Grieving is a process and takes time.

You'll want to stop for a chat whenever a child expresses interest or shows concern, during or after the reading of this book. Here are some points to keep in mind as you talk about death with a child:

1. Communicate at the child's level of understanding as much as possible.

   • Children under the age of three don't have the thinking ability needed to understand death. But they feel loss and separation. They need consistency in caregivers and routine, lots of love, and safe, friendly surroundings.

   • Children from age three through age five don't understand death either, but they have many down-to-earth questions (e.g., "Will the person have to go to the bathroom?"). They don't understand the permanence of physical death. They think that perhaps the person will come back next week.

   • Children from ages six through eight are curious as well. They know that physical death is permanent. But they have lots of questions about the details of death.

   • Symbolic explanations are difficult for all young children to understand, because they think literally.

2. Take your cues from the child. If the child seems to be keeping her feelings locked inside, encourage her to draw a picture of how she feels. Talk about the good memories you have of the one who has died. Give the child opportunities to ask questions. Let the child know that you will be there for her.

3. Try to keep other aspects of the child's life as stable as possible. Children find security and comfort when people, environments, and routines stay the same after the loss of a loved one.

4. Help the child do something in memory of the person who died. Plant a tree or a garden, make a wreath, create a scrapbook, write a poem, or make a treasure box of mementos left by the person.

5. Assure the child that death is not the end but a new beginning. It's like being born into a whole new world where there will be no more dying.

The sun comes up, and the sun goes down,

And the world keeps turning 'round and 'round.

There's a time to be born and a time to die;

A time to laugh and a time to cry.

But God is near, so I never fear,

For I walk with his hand in mine.

Gram had sung that song for as long as Anthony could remember. Sometimes she sang it when she was washing dishes. Sometimes she sang it while she was making the bed. And now she sang it when she was planting her spring garden.

"Hold out your hand," said Anthony's grandmother.

Anthony held out his hand, and Gram poured marigold seeds into his palm. "My favorite flowers," said Gram.

Anthony stared at the seeds. "They don't look like flowers," he said. "They look dead."

Gram laughed. "The part of the seed that you see is only the coat," she said. "Inside the seed, there's a special part that's alive. With a little water and some sunshine, the inside part will leave its old coat behind and grow into my favorite flower!"

A gust of wind swept a cloud over the sun and flapped the brim of Gram's gardening hat. Gram looked at the sky. It grumbled back at her with a gentle thunder.

"God is going to water our seeds, Anthony! We'd better plant them fast!" said Gram.

Anthony could smell the rain coming. He quickly dropped seeds into the long, shallow ditch that Gram drew with her finger in the dirt. Then he helped Gram cover the little ditch with more dirt. Gently they patted the dirt down. Then *plop, plop, plop.* The first big raindrops fell.

Gram took Anthony's hand as they ran
back to her house. The rain showered down
on them, but Gram said, "No matter. We'll
drip-dry."

Anthony and Gram sat in two rockers on
the covered porch. They watched the rain pour
down hard and fast. But the rain didn't last
long.

As soon as the sun peeked out again, Anthony and Gram started down the porch steps to go back to the garden. But Anthony stopped on the second step down. "Look, Gram!" he said, pointing to the edge of the step.

"Snails!" said Gram. "They've crawled up from the puddle. The rain must have filled their hole in the ground with water. Go indoors and get my magnifying glass from the table by my chair. It will help you see the snails better."

Anthony ran indoors and was back in no time with the magnifying glass. He spent the rest of the afternoon watching snails while Gram planted more flowers and sang.

The sun comes up, and the sun goes down,
And the world keeps turning 'round and 'round.
There's a time to weep and a time to dance;
A time to harvest and a time to plant.
But God is near, so I never fear,
For I walk with his hand in mine.

That summer, whenever Anthony went to see his grandmother, they spent time in the garden and looked at their favorite flowers growing full and tall. Sometimes Anthony watched snails crawl on Gram's porch steps or on the sidewalk. Other times he had to dig to find them. And once Anthony watched a snail crawl up high on the glass of the porch door.

Autumn came. A cool wind began to blow. Leaves turned orange and yellow and began to fall. At first they floated down one by one. Then they came swirling down as if the trees were shaking them off all at once. Anthony danced in the leaves as they fell.

But Gram had to watch from her window. She had become sick and very tired, so she couldn't come out to look at her garden close-up. Anthony brought her the marigolds that were still blooming. "My favorite flowers," Gram said.

"Mine too," said Anthony.

It wasn't long until the wind blew cold, sending crisp leaves skittering across the ground. Trees stretched bare, thin branches up toward the sky. The flowers in Gram's garden turned brown and dry.

Anthony sat at his kitchen table. Gram was still sick and very tired. Her flowers were all brown. He knew he couldn't pick Gram's favorite flowers for her today. So he was drawing pictures of flowers for Gram.

Anthony's mom sat down beside him. "Those are beautiful flowers," she said. "They remind me of the flowers that you helped Gram plant."

"Yes," said Anthony. "I'm drawing them for Gram. Are we still going to Gram's house today?"

"Yes," said Mom. She watched Anthony color his pictures for a minute. Then she said, "But we won't get to see Gram today."

"Why not?" asked Anthony, choosing a bright green crayon for the leaves.

Mom put her arm around Anthony's shoulders. "Gram went to the hospital in the middle of the night," said Mom. "She died before the sun came up this morning."

Anthony kept coloring. "These flowers are still for Gram," he said.

"Yes," said Mom. "And I know for a fact that Gram would love those flowers."

When Anthony finished his picture, he folded it two times and carefully put it into his pocket. He took it with him when he went with Mom and Dad to Gram's house.

Anthony wondered if Gram's house would be different without Gram. But it smelled the same. It looked the same. Gram's magnifying glass was still on the table by her big chair. So Anthony picked it up and walked outside onto the porch and down the steps. There were no snails. "Too cold for snails," said Anthony.

Anthony walked out to the garden. The flower stems stuck up straight and stiff, shivering in the cold wind. A brown, prickly knob sat on top of each stem. Anthony bent over and sniffed one to see if it had a smell.

Not much. He held Gram's magnifying glass over the prickly knob. It wasn't a flower now, but Anthony picked it anyway. The crinkly knob fell apart in his hand. Lots of little seeds tumbled out. Seeds just like the ones he and Gram had planted.

Anthony took his flower picture out of his pocket and opened it a bit. He gently dropped his handful of marigold seeds into the folds of the paper. Then Anthony slowly walked back to Gram's house.

Just before Anthony reached the porch steps, he spied something small and white, half-buried in dirt. He bent down and dug it out. It was a snail shell. But there was no snail in it. Anthony slipped the shell between the folds of his flower picture and went indoors.

Mom was sitting in Gram's big chair. "Come and sit with me, Anthony," she said.

Anthony climbed up beside Mom. He showed her the seeds and the snail shell.

"Very interesting," said Mom. She kissed Anthony on top of his head.

"Does dying hurt?" asked Anthony.

"Dying is a little bit like falling asleep to this world and waking up in a new and very special place with Jesus," said Mom. "You see, the real part of you is your spirit. That's the part of you that loves and laughs and knows things. Your spirit is who you really are deep down inside. Your body is just a house that your spirit lives in. Bodies grow old. They get sick and tired, and they die. That's what happened to Gram's body. But Gram's spirit, the real part of Gram that loves and laughs and knows things, didn't die. Gram's spirit is alive right now with Jesus."

Anthony picked up a marigold seed and looked at it carefully. "It's like the seeds," said Anthony. "The coat on the outside looks dead. But the inside will leave the coat behind and grow into a flower."

"Exactly," said Mom.

"But Gram's dying makes *me* hurt," said Anthony. "It makes me cry because I feel so sad."

"I feel sad too," said Mom. "We will miss Gram. But look at this." Mom held out the snail shell.

"The snail is not in there," Anthony said.

"But the snail has left you a treasure," said Mom. "The snail left you a beautiful white shell to keep. It's like that with people too. We can't keep forever the people we love, but they leave behind treasures that we can keep."

"What treasures did Gram leave?" asked Anthony.

"Close your eyes," said Mom. "Do you remember helping Gram plant her garden?"

Anthony nodded. He could see it in his mind: the dirt, the seeds, Gram in her gardening hat, the clouds, the rain.

"Memories are treasures that people leave with us," said Mom. "They are treasures that can never be taken away. They belong to us forever."

"What else?" asked Anthony.

"Pictures are treasures," said Mom. "We have photographs of Gram. And letters she wrote. And the recipe for her chocolate chip cookies—"

"And the magnifying glass!" said Anthony.

"Yes," said Mom. "You can keep Gram's magnifying glass as a special treasure."

"And don't forget Gram's song!" said Anthony.

"Yes!" said Mom. "We will never forget Gram's song."

Then, just to make sure he had not forgotten,
Anthony sang. And Mom joined in.

The sun comes up, and the sun goes down,

And the world keeps turning 'round and 'round.

There's a time to weep and a time to dance;

A time to harvest and a time to plant.

But God is near, so I never fear,

For I walk with his hand in mine.

The sun comes up, and the sun goes down,

And the world keeps turning 'round and 'round.

There's a time to be born and a time to die;

A time to laugh and a time to cry.

But God is near, so I never fear,

For I walk with his hand in mine.